COLIN
and the
CURLY CLAW

Jan Fearnley

Blue Bananas

For Izaak and Emily

J.F.

COLIN
and the
CURLY CLAW

First published in Great Britain 2001
This edition published in 2003
by Egmont Children's Books Limited
a division of Egmont Holding Limited
239 Kensington High Street, London W8 6SA
Published in hardback by Heinemann Library,
a division of Reed Educational and Professional Publishing Limited,
by arrangement with Egmont Books Limited.
Text and Illustrations copyright © Jan Fearnley 2001
The moral right of the author/illustrator has been asserted
Paperback ISBN 1 4052 0931 3
Hardback ISBN 0 431 06973 5
1 3 5 7 9 10 8 6 4 2
A CIP catalogue record for this title is available from the British Library.
Printed and bound in the U.A.E.

At Number 34 Eccles Street, Colin woke up

feeling very excited.

Today he was going on a trip to the museum.

Colin loved museums.

5

Colin washed his
face, even
behind his ears.

He brushed his teeth,

without being told twice!

Then he quickly got dressed.

He ate all his porridge – even the lumpy

bits – yuk!

Then he waited ages for Mum to get ready.

She was doing all that mum stuff.

At last, they set off.

The bus chugged and brummed its way

through the town until they came to the

very last stop.

The museum stop.

Mum gave Colin the money for his ticket.

He dashed up the steps. He couldn't wait to

get inside!

'Remember to say thank you,' Mum called.

The turnstile creaked as Colin pushed it

with all his might.

They went down the long, polished,

echoing corridor.

It was dark and smelt of beeswax and old

ladies' handbags.

'Don't run off,' said Mum, clumping

along behind.

11

They looked at the paintings.

They looked at the shiny suits of armour.

They looked at the Egyptian mummies.

They looked at the sculptures.

They looked at the big woolly mammoth.

It raised its trunk in salute and seemed to

point the way towards a sign . . .

TO THE DINOSAURS.

Colin sucked in his cheeks with anticipation.

His mouth made a big 'OOOH!' shape.

This was what he wanted to see more than

anything else.

15

He clattered down the dark and dusty corridor.

The dinosaurs were waiting for him.

'Not too fast!' said Mum.

Then she spotted Mrs Bakewell from down the

road and stopped to have a chat.

Colin was all alone . . .

. . . except, of course, for the dinosaurs.

Colin looked at the
dinosaur skeletons.

Big skeletons and
little skeletons and
teeny tiny skeletons.

Fat skeletons and thin skeletons and shiny,

flat fossils.

Every kind of dinosaur was there to be seen.

Flying ones, swimming ones, even ones that

moved, like they do on the television.

And there, in the corner all on its own, stood . . .

. . . the best dinosaur of all.

A powerful spotlight, as strong as the moon, lit

its yellow knobbly skin.

One big foot rested on a log, as the dinosaur

stood proudly.

Its big, bony head was held high in

the air. Its tiny eyes twinkled.

It had hundreds of dagger teeth that smiled a clever smile and on each hand there was a huge, curly claw.

It was magnificent. It was beautiful. It was so cool!

You'd better believe it, baby!

A sign said, 'Do not touch the exhibit', but Colin couldn't resist a closer look.

The dinosaur's bright eyes sparkled, the fearsome claws gleamed in the light.

Colin reached out his hand . . . and stroked one of the claws ever so gently with the tip of his finger.

And it FELL OFF!

OH NO! What have I done?

It dropped, like a big, ripe nut, right into the palm of his hand! Colin looked around. His cheeks were burning. His fingers curled around the claw. He quickly put it in his pocket and went to find his mum.

Now all he wanted was to get out of there.

Colin tried not to think about the claw but it was always there, lurking in his head.

He tried to concentrate really hard on his swimming lesson.

He worked so hard that Mum took him

to the fair as a treat. This was fantastic.

Colin began to feel a lot better.

There was just time to do some shopping for supper before they got the bus home.

By evening, Colin had almost forgotten about the claw.

But, as he swung, back and forth, back and forth, Colin was sure he could hear a strange voice calling him.

It made his hair stand on end.

who took my curly claw?
Who took my curly claw?
someone took my curly claw!
I THINK IT'S YOU!

Colin looked around. There was nobody

to be seen.

I must have imagined it.

The voice growled again . . .

who took my curly claw?

Who took my curly claw?

someone took my curly claw!

I THINK IT'S YOU!

Colin ran up the garden path and

hammered on the door.

He could still hear the voice . . . it was

following him!

Oh, no!

Who took my curly claw?
Who took my curly claw?
Someone took my curly claw!
I THINK IT'S YOU!

Mum opened the door. Colin dashed in.

'Thanks very much, I'm sure,' Mum said.

Colin sprinted up the stairs, fast as a whippet.

Thud, thud, thud, went his feet.

Boom diddy boom went his heart.

And all the time, that voice was getting closer . . .

Colin reached his room and dived under the duvet.

All the time, the voice was calling . . .

Colin tucked the covers right over his head.

Now there were footsteps on the stairs, the slow, careful tread of something big coming to gobble him up!

The door opened . . . CREEEAAAK!

It was Mum!

'I thought you were a dinosaur!' Colin cried.

Once in bed, Colin reached under the quilt

and gave Mum the curly claw.

'It's a real dinosaur claw,' he said in a

small voice.

'Very nice dear,' said Mum, putting the

claw in her pocket.

'We'll take it back tomorrow.'

Colin sighed and settled down. Mum

read a story.

'Goodnight,' she said when they got to

the end.

After a long bath, Mum popped the claw into the pocket of her favourite dressing-gown and went downstairs.

'Dinosaurs indeed!' She chuckled to herself. 'That boy has such an imagination.'

He's always making things up.

She made herself a mug of cocoa.

She got herself a biscuit.

And settled down for the evening.

The next day, the curator of the museum was very cross.

'What has happened to my best exhibit?' he said.

He took my dressing-gown!

Where **did** those clothes come from?

The dinosaur didn't move but he seemed to
be standing even prouder than usual, from
the top of his noble head right down to the
tips of his nicely painted claws.

The dinosaur was even **more** popular than ever! Only Colin and his mum knew exactly what had **happened**.

But *they* weren't **going** to tell, not ever.